# The
# Crumbly
# Coast

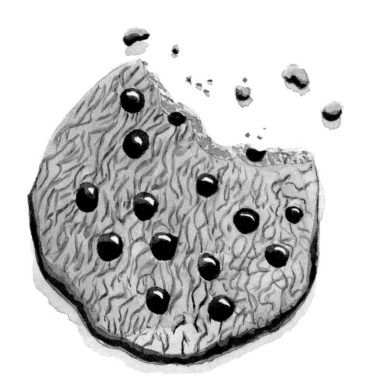

# The
# Crumbly
# C🍪ast

## DAVID LYON

*A Doubleday Book for Young Readers*

Olivia Smith and her live mink, Slinky, were driving along the coast in Olivia's sports car.

After several hours, they stopped at a small roadside cafe for a snack.

The cafe was owned and operated by the Home Away from Home Orphanage. Inside, an orphan greeted them at the door.

"A table for two, please," said Olivia.

"I'm sorry, no pets are allowed," said the orphan.

"I'm no pet," said Slinky. "I'm a wrap. Do you have a rule against wraps?"

"No, we don't," said the orphan, with a smile.

"Thank goodness," said Olivia.

The orphan showed Olivia and Slinky to their table.

"Two glasses of milk," said Olivia.

"And two big cookies!" said Slinky.

At this, the orphan began to cry. A woman named Betty came running out of the kitchen. She hugged the orphan.

"What's wrong?" Betty asked.

"All we did was order some cookies," said Slinky.

"Oh," said Betty. "You see, someone stole our cookies this morning!"

"That's okay. Some chocolate cake would be fine," said Slinky.

"Slinky!" said Olivia. Then she turned to Betty.

"We'll help you catch those cookie thieves!" Olivia said.

"That would be very nice," said Betty. The orphan started drying her eyes with her sleeve.

"Here, use my tail," said Slinky.

"You're very kind," said the orphan.

Betty took Olivia and Slinky to the back of the restaurant, where they met the other orphans. The orphans showed Olivia and Slinky where they had last seen their cookies.

Olivia noticed some fur caught on a rosebush, and Slinky spotted footprints and cookie crumbs leading off into the woods.

"We shall follow those footsteps!" said Olivia.

"Wherever they may lead," said Slinky.

"Please be careful," said Betty.

"If it's convenient," said Slinky, a determined look in his eyes.

Olivia and Slinky set off right away. The trail was easy to follow. The footprints were large and deep, and a line of brightly colored birds had formed, eating the crumbs the cookie thieves had dropped.

Just as the sun was beginning to set, Olivia and Slinky spotted a campfire flickering upon a mountaintop. Around the fire stood a circle of bears, murmuring, chanting, and waving their arms, while a three-piece band played a strange but compelling tune.

Olivia and Slinky snuck up close to the bears. Suddenly, an old bear stood and cleared his throat. His name was Horatio and he was the old bear mythmaker.

"It is time," he said, "to recall the teachings of Umlo, the Magic Bear—the bear who taught us how to find the cookies of our dreams."

Then he held out his arms and spoke:

Go, old bear, who cookie seeks,
Downwards to that crumbly beach,
Where stands a building painted peach,
And bakers singing, each to each.

Oh, there those tasty Kookies be!
Rounded orbs of chewy joy!
Lumpadough, baked just so!
Umpa dumpa, umpadumpa-doo!

At this point, all the bears bounced on their left feet, and then their right feet, and then spun around.

Then Horatio cried, "Bring out the cookies!" and a large bear dressed in a fancy hat brought out a plateful of cookies and began to pass them around. Suddenly, Olivia and Slinky stood up.

"Not so fast," said Slinky. "Those cookies don't belong to you."

"No," said Olivia. "Those cookies belong to the little boys and girls of the Home Away from Home Orphanage."

"Orphanage?" asked one bear.

"Little boys and girls?" asked another.

"That's ridiculous," said the bear in the hat. "These cookies were baked for us by little troll bakers on the beach, just like Umlo the Magic Bear taught us."

"That's a nice little story," said Slinky, "but it doesn't fit the facts. You bears have stolen cookies from eight little orphans!"

Olivia showed the bears photographs of the orphans and a promotional brochure for the orphanage. She also showed them photos of cookies which looked very similar to the ones the bears were now eating. The bears were very upset and argued among themselves.

Several of the bears thought that Olivia and Slinky just wanted the cookies for themselves. Other bears argued that they were just making things up. Some bears thought Olivia and Slinky were crazy!

"I think that maybe we should send somebody back with our guests and make sure that a terrible mistake has not been made," said a soft-spoken bear.

Finally, a vote was taken. The bears decided to send a fact-finding commission to make further investigations.

The next morning, three bears went with Olivia and Slinky to the orphanage. Olivia introduced the bears to Betty and the orphans, and gave them a tour. The three bears quickly realized a mistake had been made.

"We thought you were little troll bakers," they explained. Then they apologized for their mistake and returned what was left of the cookies.

The orphans accepted the bears' apology. They even invited the bears to lunch. After a delicious meal, the bears went home, and Betty thanked Olivia and Slinky.

"It was nothing," said Slinky, polishing his magnifying glass.

That day the children had a few cookies in the afternoon. It was good to be eating cookies again! Nevertheless, many of the children felt bad that the bears had no cookies for their festival.

The orphans began their own debate. Some children argued that they should share the cookies. Some argued that they should keep the cookies. And some argued that they should forget about cookies altogether and talk about the world political situation.

Finally, the orphans came to a decision. They would share their cookies with the bears! Betty, Olivia, and Slinky were very impressed.

After a busy afternoon of baking, everyone climbed into Olivia's car and drove to the top of the mountain.

When they arrived, it was a very sad scene. There was no campfire and no band. No bears were dancing, except for a bear named Elizabeth, and it turned out that she had just stubbed her toe.

Many of the bears were sitting around chewing on old
roots. Some were even eating bugs and the leaves off of
bushes!

Horatio, the old bear mythmaker, was hiding behind a rock. He had never seen a car or little boys and girls before.

"Look!' he cried. "A spaceship full of aliens!"

"Oh, no, it's the orphans!" shouted the bears who had returned the cookies. They ran up to their visitors and gave them big bear hugs.

The orphans smiled and showed the bears the cookies they had baked that afternoon. "These are for your festival," they explained.

"Whoopah!" shouted the bears in a joyous bear cry.
Then the annual wild bear cookie festival really began,
with dancing and whooping and hollering and a great
sharing of cookies.

When it was very late, everyone said good-bye. Olivia and Slinky drove Betty and the orphans back to the orphanage.

And even before the taillights of Olivia's car had disappeared around the bend, Horatio, the old bear mythmaker, was busy telling the story of the alien spaceship that brought cookies from the stars.

A Doubleday Book for Young Readers
Published by Delacorte Press
Bantam Doubleday Dell Publishing Group, Inc.
1540 Broadway
New York, New York 10036
Doubleday and the portrayal of an anchor with a dolphin are trademarks of
Bantam Doubleday Dell Publishing Group, Inc.

Library of Congress Cataloging in Publication Data
Lyon, David.
The crumbly coast/David Lyon.
p.    cm.
Summary: Olivia and her mink Slinky find the bears who have stolen cookies from
the orphans, but then the orphans become concerned that the bears cannot
celebrate their annual cookie festival.
ISBN 0-385-32079-5
[1. Bears—Fiction.   2. Minks—Fiction.   3. Orphans—Fiction.
4. Cookies—Fiction.]   I. Title.
Pz7.L99528Cr   1995
[E]—dc20
93-41083   CIP   AC

Manufactured in the United States of America

August 1995
10  9  8  7  6  5  4  3  2  1